# PEANUTS

# Snoopy Takes Off!

By Charles M. Schulz

Adapted by Tina Gallo

Illustrated by Scott Jeralds

SIMON SPOTLIGHT

New York   London   Toronto   Sydney   New Delhi

SIMON SPOTLIGHT
An imprint of Simon & Schuster Children's Publishing Division
1230 Avenue of the Americas, New York, New York 10020
This Simon Spotlight hardcover edition August 2016
© 2015 Peanuts Worldwide L.L.C.
SIMON SPOTLIGHT and colophon are registered trademarks of Simon & Schuster, Inc.
For information about special discounts for bulk purchases, please contact Simon & Schuster
Special Sales at 1-866-506-1949 or business@simonandschuster.com.
Manufactured in China 0616 SCP
10 9 8 7 6 5 4 3 2 1
ISBN 978-1-4814-6929-6 (hc)
ISBN 978-1-4814-2554-4 (pbk)
ISBN 978-1-4814-2555-1 (eBook)

This is Snoopy. He may look like a regular dog to you, but in fact, he is anything but ordinary!

Snoopy doesn't do anything the same way as an ordinary dog, starting with the way he sleeps *on* his doghouse, rather than inside.

Charlie Brown is Snoopy's owner, although a lot of the time it seems like it's the other way around.

What a beautiful day, Snoopy thinks. It's a perfect day for me to jump in my plane, soar through the air, and fight the Red Baron!

When Snoopy says he is going to "jump in his plane," he really means he's going to sit on top of his doghouse. He puts on his goggles, scarf, and helmet. "Here's the World War One Flying Ace flying across the sky in his Sopwith Camel airplane," Snoopy says. "Where are you, Red Baron? You can't hide from me!"

Suddenly Snoopy spots the Red Baron's plane! "Yes!" he cheers. He is finally going to capture the enemy!

"Full speed ahead!" Snoopy shouts. But as fast as Snoopy is, the Red Baron is faster. He gets away . . . again. "Noooo!" Snoopy shouts, waving his fist. "I'll get you, Red Baron! Next time you are mine!"

Snoopy takes off his helmet and sits down with a sigh. He turns around and sees Charlie Brown standing with his food dish. Charlie Brown is shaking his head.

"I wonder what it would be like to have a normal dog," Charlie Brown tells him.

Snoopy ignores him and concentrates on enjoying his food. Being a World War I Flying Ace works up an appetite!

Later that afternoon Snoopy is bored, so he decides to write the next Great American Novel. He pulls out his trusty old typewriter and begins to write.

It was a dark and stormy night.

Linus walks by and is curious. "May I see what you've written?" he asks.

Snoopy nods and hands Linus the page.

"Your new novel has a very exciting beginning," Linus says.

Snoopy smiles proudly.

Linus hands back the sheet of paper. "Well, good luck with the second sentence," he says.

Lucy is curious about Snoopy's book too. She has a suggestion for him. "'It was a dark and stormy night' is a terrible way to begin a story," she says. "You should begin your story with 'Once upon a time.' That's the way all good stories begin."

Snoopy thinks Lucy may be right, so he changes the beginning of his story. He types:

# Once upon a time, it was a dark and stormy night.

Lucy looks at the new sheet of paper and groans.
"Can't you write about something nice?" she asks Snoopy.

Snoopy thinks this is a good idea. So he types. Then he stops typing, and to Lucy's surprise, he jumps off his doghouse . . .

Once upon a time, it was a dark and stormy night. Suddenly, a kiss rang out!

and he gives Lucy a big kiss!

"Aaagh, I've been kissed by a dog! I've got dog germs!" Lucy cries, and runs away.

*That wasn't nearly as romantic as I thought it would be,* Snoopy thinks.

Snoopy decides it's time for a dance break! There's nothing Snoopy loves more than dancing!

He dances with Charlie Brown!

He dances with Lucy!

He dances with Linus!

He even dances on top of Schroeder's piano! (Schroeder doesn't like this very much.)

After all that dancing, it's time for a snack. Snoopy invites his best friend, Woodstock, to come over for some homemade cookies and milk. Even though Snoopy enjoys the dog food Charlie Brown brings him, he is also a fabulous cook, and loves whipping up surprises for his friends.

Woodstock loves hanging out with Snoopy and tells him all about his day. Fortunately for Woodstock, Snoopy is fluent in bird and understands every word he says.

Woodstock wants to go on a camping trip with Snoopy and some of his friends.

"That's a great idea!" Snoopy says. "After all, I *am a* Beagle Scout!"

Woodstock quickly gathers his friends.

"Follow me, troops," Snoopy says. "And I don't want to see anyone hanging around my feet!"

The birds are very nervous about the hike. They want to stay as close to Snoopy as possible, so they all fly onto the top of his Beagle Scout hat. *Well, at least they paid attention to some of what I said,* Snoopy thinks.

It isn't long before the birds get very homesick, so Snoopy decides to cut the trip short. "It's the perfect time to head home," Snoopy tells them. They knock on Charlie Brown's door. "We're just in time for dinner."

"Well, I guess now you probably just want to relax for a while," Charlie Brown says.

Snoopy looks at him in shock. Relax? Is he kidding? Snoopy pulls out a guitar. It's time for a little after-dinner music!

"I guess you'll never be an ordinary dog, will you, Snoopy?" Charlie Brown says. "But you know what? I don't think I'd have it any other way."

*Neither would I!* Snoopy thinks happily. *Neither would I!*